W9-ACE-233

Across the RAINBOW

A HARMONY INK PRESS ANTHOLOGY

Harmony Ink

Published by
HARMONY INK PRESS

5032 Capital Circle SW, Suite 2, PMB# 279, Tallahassee, FL 32305-7886 USA
publisher@harmonyinkpress.com • http://harmonyinkpress.com

This is a work of fiction. Names, characters, places, and incidents either are the product of author imagination or are used fictitiously, and any resemblance to actual persons, living or dead, business establishments, events, or locales is entirely coincidental.

Across the Rainbow
© 2014 Harmony Ink Press.
Edited by Anne Regan

American Spanish © 2014 Gene Gant.
Choices © 2014 John Goode.
Eric's Secret © 2014 Sam Kadence.
The Most Beautiful Boy in the Whole World © 2014 Amy Lane.
Summer with Adeline © 2014 Zoe Lynne.
Faking Truth © 2014 Jo Ramsey.

Cover Art
© 2014 Paul Richmond.
http://www.paulrichmondstudio.com
Cover content is for illustrative purposes only and any person depicted on the cover is a model.

All rights reserved. This book is licensed to the original purchaser only. Duplication or distribution via any means is illegal and a violation of international copyright law, subject to criminal prosecution and upon conviction, fines, and/or imprisonment. Any eBook format cannot be legally loaned or given to others. No part of this book may be reproduced or transmitted in any form or by any means, electronic or mechanical, including photocopying, recording, or by any information storage and retrieval system, without the written permission of the Publisher, except where permitted by law. To request permission and all other inquiries, contact Harmony Ink Press, 5032 Capital Circle SW, Suite 2, PMB# 279, Tallahassee, FL 32305-7886, USA, or publisher@harmonyinkpress.com.

ISBN: 978-1-63216-940-2
Library of Congress Control Number: 2014953647
First Edition November 2014

Printed in the United States of America

This paper meets the requirements of
ANSI/NISO Z39.48-1992 (Permanence of Paper).

Table of Contents

HARMONY INK Press publishes young adult fiction featuring positive LGBTQ+ characters. Whether teens are gay, lesbian, bisexual, transgender, asexual, intersex, genderfluid, or still searching for their sexual and gender identity, our goal is to present books with characters like themselves, characters who face the challenges and issues they do and grow through their experiences.

Since our founding in 2012, Harmony Ink has published stories by over eighty authors. We release a new title every Thursday, ranging from contemporary romance to fantasy, science fiction, mystery, paranormal, and historical genres. We also sponsor our annual Young Author Challenge, looking for the best short LGBTQ+ fiction by writers between the ages of fourteen to twenty-one.

This volume features six of Harmony Ink's most popular authors, providing a sample of the variety of fiction we publish. Additional information, including new releases, story excerpts, author interviews, calls for submission (including the Young Author Challenge), and more, can be found on our website, www.harmonyinkpress.com.

Enjoy this trip across the rainbow with Harmony Ink Press.

Anne Regan
Executive Editor
November 2014

Choices

JOHN GOODE

I DIDN'T choose to have black hair.

If anyone had asked me, I would have chosen blond, or maybe that sandy brown that looks so freaking cute on guys. Instead I got boring black, which made me look even duller than I already was. Bad enough that I was Middle Eastern, so everyone looked at me when they thought I couldn't tell, but the black hair just made it so stereotypical that I could scream. I hated it, but it was the hair I got.

I didn't choose to have brown eyes.

Which, by the way, are the worst color eyes ever. If I could choose, I would have picked, like, blue or green, of course, but if I could have anything? Gray. A smoky gray that just screamed mystery at you. Instead I got crap brown, which made no one look into my eyes and wonder what I was thinking. It made them look into my eyes and go, "Oh, it's him." I didn't pick them, and I wish I could have.

I didn't choose to be short.

Being short sucks balls for many reasons. One, because guys are supposed to be tall. It's, like, a guy thing, so when you aren't, people's first thought is that you're not a complete man. I mean, not in that way, of course. I mean in a manly man way. If you're short you're automatically lesser in people's eyes, and there's nothing you can do to change their mind. Try to be forceful? You're just a short guy with 'tude. Act the same way at six foot two, and you're Superman. I hate it, and worse, there's nothing to do about it. I've heard of this messed-up thing where they break your legs and it heals and it's supposed to make you taller, but screw that. I mean, if someone is going to break my legs, I better owe them lots of money, you know? So no, didn't choose it, hate it with a passion.

I didn't choose to be fat.

Okay, fine, I'm not fat but I am not skinny. I'm one of those pleasantly plump people who are not pleasant about it at all. I've tried the diet thing and the exercise thing, but no matter what I do, I'm wide. Of course I'd rather be perfect and toned and all that—who wouldn't? I look at people like that and shake my head. Where do they come from? What do they eat? I know it's just genetics, but that is some X-Men crap right there, because it doesn't look real. So no, don't like being big, but there I am. What are you gonna do about it?

I didn't choose to be Islamic.

No one asked me when I was born if I wanted to worship a God that would make people want to kill me. No one asked if I wanted to look like a group of fanatics who flew planes into buildings in the name of my God. No one asked me if I felt the same way they did or if I cried when I saw the smoke coming from the buildings. No one did and I hate it. Not the religion, the people who tainted it for the rest of the world. And by the way, if I could have chosen, I would have loved the same God no matter who else worshiped him.

I didn't choose to be shy.

There was no buffet of social skills laid out to me before I was born, where I could pick and choose what kind of personality I would have. I didn't get a say that I can't talk in public or that I hate confrontation to the point where I will just walk away rather than defend myself sometimes. If I could have picked, I would have taken some of Zac Efron's positivity with a little of Chace Crawford's swag. Maybe a little of Miley's ability not to care and just a smidgen of Harry Styles's sexiness. But no one offered so I'm just shy, boring me.

I didn't choose to be gay.

I know, duh, but some people seem to think we do. I was born gay, and I know it 'cause when other guys were out there licking frogs or playing in the mud or whatever straight boys do, I was with my sisters having tea with our stuffed animals. When I was six, I asked Bobby Walker to be my boyfriend. I want to point out he said sure, though that was most likely because I had Oreos, but whatever—he said yes. I was never attracted to girls and never tried to be. This was me and that was it. I no more thought about sleeping with girls than the straight boys thought about sleeping with boys. It was how I was born and that was the way it was. I was gay and I love it.

Because it's me.

There are a lot of things I wish I could be. Taller, blonder, funnier, sexier… but never once have I ever wanted to be not me. Because there's not another me out there. I am unique, which means that if I were to cease to exist, there would be a shocking lack of me in the world. You're the same way. You are you and that is incredible, because there isn't another you. And if you spend time wanting to be someone else—don't. Because if you were that person, then there'd be two of them and none of you, and that would suck.

Because there isn't enough you in the world.

There isn't enough me.

So let's do something about that, okay?

JOHN GOODE is a member of the class of '88 from Hogwarts School of Witchcraft and Wizardry, specializing in incantations and spoken spells. At the age of fourteen, he proudly represented District 13 in the 65th Panem games, where he was disqualified for crying uncontrollably before the competition began. After that he moved to Forks, Washington, where against all odds he dated the hot, incredibly approachable werewolf instead of the stuck-up jerk of a vampire, but was crushed when he found out the werewolf was actually gayer than he was. After that he turned down the mandatory operation everyone must receive at sixteen to become pretty, citing that everyone pretty was just too stupid to live, before moving away for greener pastures. After falling down an oddly large rabbit hole, he became huge when his love for cakes combined with his inability to resist the commands of sparsely worded notes, and was finally kicked out when he began playing solitaire with the Red Queen's 4th Armored Division. By eighteen he had found the land in the back of his wardrobe, but decided that thinly veiled religious allegories were not the neighbors he desired. When last seen, he had become obsessed with growing a pair of wings after discovering Fang's blog and hasn't been seen since.

Or he is this guy who lives in this place and writes stuff he hopes you read.

Summer with Adeline

ZOE LYNNE

FROM THE bay window of my bedroom, I spied as a U-Haul pulled into the driveway next door. My house crowned the cul-de-sac, a manicured jewel and testament to my parents' hard work. We'd lived there forever, and I'd seen many people come and go over the years, lost plenty of friends to sudden, unexplained moves. A similar tragedy had befallen the house next door.

It was huge and once outshone mine. Its peaks rose well above my home's and pitched shadows over our yard. There were even spots where the grass never grew because the sunlight couldn't clear its roof. The place was beautiful, though, and so freaking mysterious I would sit in my bedroom window conjuring stories about vampires and witches. I never thought someone would actually move into the old thing. Then the construction crews showed up and dark and dreary became light and colorful. Even the yard had been decorated with a magical rainbow parade of flowers.

My stories changed the moment the men tore off the first shingle. I imagined a princess hidden away in the room across from mine, waiting to be handed over to her prince, when she only wanted to love her handmaiden. She would spend hours watching the other girl tend to her duties, but when it came time for bathing, the princess was at her happiest.

A mountain of a man rose up from the cab of the U-Haul. He unfolded himself, much like a circus clown with stilts for legs climbing out of a tiny car. He was a giant, lean and tall, with skin the color of my favorite candy bar. Long braids hung down his back. His muscles nearly bulged out of his shirt. I gasped at the sight of him. I would've bet he could tear any mortal man limb from limb.

The woman who pulled up in the car behind him had the longest, silkiest ebony hair I'd ever seen and eyes the shape of almonds. Like maybe she was Asian or… or something. I didn't know and certainly didn't want to offend by assuming. "She's beautiful," I said with a gasp, and not just pretty like a mother would be, but fairytale beautiful. She was the queen, clearly. She was exotic and intriguing and no one in the suburbs looked like she did.

"But where's the princess?" I whined. I hated when my voice did that.

I kept watching, hoping and praying the princess would appear. People came and went. They moved things in and out of the house. Apparently old furniture had been left behind and its new home was on the curb with the trash. I saw them bring in furniture that could've been for a girl's room, but I still didn't see the princess. No matter how long I watched and waited, she never appeared.

THE NEW family had lived next door for a few months, and they hadn't spoken to anyone in the neighborhood. I'd heard my mom and her Nosy Nancy gossip circle conjuring all kinds of stories about them. Mine were better. My stories didn't involve crime syndicates and grand conspiracies. Mine were all fun and fantastic. Fairy tales with happily ever afters. But then, the stories just sort of stopped. When I realized I'd been waiting for a new friend who would never come, I lost interest.

It was the end of school, the very last stop the bus would make in my neighborhood until summer came to an end and the first day of my junior year began. I'd said good-bye to my friends with promises of meeting up tomorrow to go swimming at the community center, and that's when I saw her.

The princess had finally arrived.

I couldn't pick a famous face to compare her to because I'd never seen anyone who looked like her. She was tall like the man with the braids and thin like the woman with the almond eyes. Her body was both toned and lithe, strong and elegant. But her face drew me in. Her pointed chin and high cheeks reminded me of the fairy princesses from my childhood. I'd always wanted to look like that, and I pictured the girl I fell in love with looking just like those colorful, winged creatures of my favorite tales.

There wasn't a single boy on this planet who had made me feel the way she did in a matter of seconds. It wasn't about sex or anything like that. More about seeing someone and just knowing they were going to be epically special to you. But what were the chances she looked at girls the same way I did? Slim. Probably none.

She smiled, and I would've sworn the whole world lit up, that the sun burned brighter and the birds chirped louder. She was one of those girls who walked into a room and everything stopped, like time froze for everyone but her. I'd stopped moving too. Just like time. I'd been standing there staring long enough for the bus to have become nothing but a cloud of exhaust and the friends I'd been laughing and smiling with to have disappeared. It was just us now. And she was still freakin' smiling.

Oh. Em. Gee.

I did what I always did when I noticed any sort of attention turned my way: compulsively tucked my hair behind my ear to hide my face while watching her through the part in my fingers, and I speed-walked all the way to my driveway. Like *that* wasn't obvious. *Pft.*

"Hey."

Forget the birds. Her voice sounded like an angel's song.

I froze again, slowly turned on my heel, and hesitantly raised my head.

She was *still* smiling.

I couldn't utter the first syllable.

She approached me, walking with poise and confidence. She had the biggest stride and the longest legs, tall and slender. She was probably a cheerleader or a runner or maybe even both. And what was I? Drama nerd? Vice president of the literary club? Soooooo tragically unpopular I wasn't worthy of the cool kids' jokes?

"I'm Adeline, but my friends all call me Addy."

"What am I supposed to call you?" I blurted without thinking, and of course, the facepalm normal people did as a mental expression, I physically enacted on my forehead. I winced. It stung.

She flinched, sobered, then reached out to me. "Are you okay?"

Clearly not. I was a social idiot. Awkward didn't even really describe me. It was just... bad. As comical as it sounded, the situation was anything but. I'd made a total ass out of myself in front of the most gorgeous girl I'd ever seen.

"You can call me Addy," she said. "Because I have a feeling we're totes gonna be friends."

I sighed. Yes, definitely had to be a cheerleader. I hated that stupid mallspeak all the girls and guys my age were using. Which was one more thing that made me a nerd. It wasn't bad enough I wore glasses and had braces. I didn't speak the lingo either.

"What's your name?" she asked.

"River. River Torres." And *that* was another.

Unlike all the other times I introduced myself to people—normal people—Addy didn't laugh. She didn't ask me if my parents were hippies. They were, but still....

"I like it." Addy beamed.

I melted.

"Sooo...." She looked over my shoulder, then back at me. Her eyes reminded me of caramel dropped on two perfectly shaped almonds. "Do you go to Radcliffe? What grade will you be in?"

"I, um… I do." Again with the nervous stuff. I lowered my head, tucking back hair that hadn't fallen. "I'll be a junior."

"Me too!" she squealed. "Maybe we can have lunch together."

Lunch. Ha. I almost snorted. At Radcliffe she would fall in with the popular kids, and popular kids didn't eat lunch with nerds.

I opened my mouth to say something kind, something that wouldn't make her think I was a big ol' ball of insecurity, when I heard my mother calling my name. I swung around, long frizzy brown curls beating me about the face. *Thank you, physics.*

My mother smiled, wringing her hands with a towel. From the looks of it, she'd been elbow-deep in clay. And oh em gee, she was coming this way.

I panicked; heat rushed into my face. If there was one thing my amazingly inspiring mother was good at, it was embarrassing the crap out of me, and in front of the pretty new neighbor too. I wanted to die.

"Hi," she said, extending her moderately clean and slightly discolored arm. "I'm Flora, River's mother."

"Nice to meet you, Mrs. Torres." Addy actually took her hand. I couldn't believe it. I would've taken one look at the clay and gagged. But the princess donned a beautifully pleasant smile and introduced herself. "I'm Adeline."

"Her friends call her Addy," I muttered.

"I was just about to make a plate of fresh veggies from the garden for River," my mother said, ignoring my obvious displeasure. "Would you like to join us?"

"No," I blurted. "I have homework."

"But it's the last day of school."

"Summer reading list."

Mom and Addy both laughed like I'd told some ridiculously funny joke. Heat poured into my face again. I was so embarrassed all I could do was walk away.

I left my mother and the star of my fairy tale standing in the driveway while I ran into the house and charged upstairs to my bedroom. I went straight to the window so I could keep watching her—her sincere smile, the twinkle in her caramel eyes, the way the wind ruffled her hair and the way it always fell right back into place. I imagined her pink lips curling at the edge just before she touched them to mine. I wanted to be her handmaiden and her my princess.

That night, I pulled my journal out of its secret spot. I hadn't touched it in months and some of the jewels had fallen off, leaving behind crusty rings where pink gems once adorned brighter pink silk. My mother and I had made those journals the summer before seventh grade. Hers was sage and held mementos of my childhood. Mine was every imaginable shade of pink and held stories from my overactive imagination.

I took my favorite hot pink pen to the rough pages, and I wrote.

Every single day for the next six weeks, Addy and I were pretty much inseparable. In the beginning, each encounter started awkwardly like our first meeting. I didn't say much, and Addy turned up the charm. I would find myself staring at her lips while she spoke, wondering if I would ever know what they tasted like. I'd never been kissed before and wanted so badly for her to be my first. And every single night, before I went to bed, I sat in my window and waited for the princess to come up to her room. I prayed she didn't catch me there. She never did. We became best friends, shared all our hopes and dreams, shared all our secrets… save for one.

I never told Addy what I thought when I looked at her or how I dreamed about cuddling with her or watching the stars float across the galaxy on a summer night with her. I never told her about the story of the princess or how badly I wanted to kiss her.

Then came the last day of our summer break….

I KNEW after today my relationship with Addy wouldn't be the same. Yeah, she swore we would be friends at school too, and part of me wanted to believe that was true. But I knew better. At Radcliffe the lines between cliques were clearly drawn and never shall they intermingle. I knew as soon as the popular girls got their mitts on my Addy, that chapter of my life would close, and I would have to chalk her up as the one who got away.

I sat on the edge of the swimming pool, watching Addy practice her breaststroke. Actually, I was staring at the ripples in the water as her lithe body moved through it, while pondering the end of our summer friendship-relationship thingy. Whatever it was. I debated over and over coming clean or staying in the closet. The situation could go one of two ways. She could out me to the school, and not only would I be a nerd, but I'd be "the lesbian" too. Or, I could keep my feelings to myself and pretend summer with Addy never happened. The latter felt wrong, but the other option had a monumentally detrimental outcome—one I knew I wasn't strong enough to survive.

So later that afternoon, after all the day's fun had come to an end and it was time to get serious about going back to school, I turned to her and said, "Hey, Addy, I have something I want to give you."

"Presents! Yay!"

Her enthusiasm was so contagious. It felt right to give her this gift.

I handed over the sparkling pink ode to my love affair with her house and the princess within its walls and silently prayed I hadn't made the biggest mistake of my life. Upside, if she understood it, she wasn't as vapid and brain-dead as the people she would no doubt become friends with. Downside, if she understood it, then I'd put myself out there, and God only knew the repercussions from that.

"Wait 'til you get home to read it, please."

"I promise."

"River, time for dinner," Mom called up the stairs. It was the first time in fifteen forevers that I was thankful for my mother's unwavering need to have us sit down at the dinner table together, because it broke me away from the dread and certain doom I knew I was now facing.

Addy left and I went to the table. Throughout dinner my mind was with her, wondering if she'd read the journal or if giving it to her was a waste. My parents chastised me for not eating, telling me things like "think of the starving children of the world" and all that. I always thought of the starving children, never left a crumb on my plate because of the starving children. But right now, I wanted to think about Addy.

I went through my normal postdinner routine: helping Mom clean up, shower, backpack ready for tomorrow. Truthfully, I wasn't looking forward to going back to school, because I wasn't ready for Addy to figure out the awful truth about me. I wasn't ready to mark the death of the most wonderful six weeks of my life.

Curiosity eventually got the best of me. I peeked out my window and over to hers.

Through the sheers I saw her sitting at her vanity with my journal in her hands. From where I stood, I could tell she'd read a lot of it, and it didn't look like she had any interest in stopping. Through the reflection in her vanity mirror, I saw her watery eyes and the glistening tracks rolling down her cheeks. She'd been crying. My story made her cry.

"Oh no," I gasped. That wasn't the purpose of sharing it.

"Addy!" I called out. She didn't hear me. How could she with double-paned glass and ten feet of air between us? I pushed open my window and put as much of my body onto the ledge as I could without falling out.

"Adeline!" She didn't lift her head. I waved my arms in the air, desperately fighting to get her attention. When she finally looked up, I blew out a breath.

"Go outside," I yelled, vehemently stabbing my finger toward the ground.

She nodded and then disappeared.

My heart nearly leapt out of my chest. My brain was so jumbled it didn't send the signal to my feet to get moving. Not as quickly as it needed to. When I did finally get going, I ran down the steps so fast I was surprised I didn't fall flat on my face. I tore out the front door and there she was, hugging my journal to her chest.

"It wasn't supposed to make you cry," I said, fighting to catch my breath. It burned.

"It was beautiful." She sighed like a girl swooning over her first crush. "And the princess loves the handmaiden very, very much."

"I—" My mouth stopped moving, jaw slack. I couldn't make words. Where I was once an intelligent person, I had nothing. No sentences. No quips. A bunch of thoughts with no way to articulate them. That's called shock, right? The best I could do was blink.

Did she just say what I thought she said?

"Wait. What?"

She didn't answer me. Not with words. Suddenly there was no space left between us and her lips were on mine. Her eyes were closed while I stared in utter disbelief. But when the shock wore off and I realized everything I'd been wishing for was finally coming true, that I was getting my fairy tale, I closed my eyes, and I let myself feel the most magical experience of my adolescence.

The princess was kissing me. Me! The nerdy handmaiden with the crush.

ZOE LYNNE strives to give LGBT youth stories they love, with heroes they can relate to. Zoe Lynne began in October of 2012, with the sole focus being to create books with LGBT youth in mind. It is Zoe Lynne's hope to deliver characters who are both real and fantastic, characters you love and love to hate, but more so, characters you can relate to. The author behind Zoe Lynne has received accolades in adult romance.

Find more from Zoe Lynne at http://zoelynnebooks.blogspot.com; follow her on Facebook: https://www.facebook.com/ZoeLynneBooks or Twitter: https://twitter.com/ZoeLynneBooks; or e-mail her at author@ zoelynnebooks.com.

American Spanish

GENE GANT

LIAM MASON got into trouble throwing a party, which would not be news if you knew Liam. This was trouble on multiple levels—epic, even.

Start with the party itself. He threw the thing when his parents headed down to the Tunica casinos for the weekend to celebrate their wedding anniversary. He didn't ask their permission, of course. Then there's the fact that he raided the family's stash of emergency cha-ching and paid an adult neighbor—a twenty-one-year-old college junior with actual state-issued ID—fifty bucks to buy five cases of beer along with several bottles of whiskey and vodka. On top of that, every one of the twenty-eight people he invited was under the age of eighteen, and many of them showed up with their own invitees. There were also illegal drugs, mostly the kind you roll up and smoke, but also the kind you spread out in a line on a flat surface and snort up your nose. So on the hot Friday night before Labor Day, in the quiet suburban town of Collierville, Tennessee, about sixty kids partied at the Masons' house. They got drunk, they got stoned, they got wild, and they got loud.

You can see where this was going.

I'm not a party guy. I don't like big gatherings, at least not the interactive kind. I'm fine at movie theaters and sports arenas, where the crowd is there to watch a show. Amusement parks are doable for me because everybody is on rides and screaming their lungs out. But I'm not good at the kind of function where people get together to talk with each other, dance with each other, sneak off into closets and make out with each other. Aside from Liam, I didn't really know anybody at the party, and I never know what to say to people I don't know. I can't dance. And nobody's ever tried to make out with me. I'm also scared to death of alcohol and drugs.

So how did I wind up at Liam's party? He invited me. He walked up behind me Friday afternoon while I was at my locker grabbing stuff for the last class of the day and said, "Hey, man. Party at my house tonight. You're coming."

"Uh… no, I'm not. Thanks for asking, Liam, but no."

"Come on, man. You never really hang out. You miss out on everything."

I shrugged and wondered how many other ways there were to say no.

He gave me that cocky smirk the girls liked so much. "You can't say no, Dale. You're coming."

"How would I get to your place? I'd have to get my mom or dad to drop me off, and they're gonna want to make sure your parents are there for this party, and I'm guessing your parents *won't* be home." I figured that would get me out of it. The last thing Liam would want is my parents getting in touch with his parents about his plans.

"Call your folks and tell 'em you're hanging with me after school," he replied smoothly. "They won't mind, and you won't be lying about what you're doing. I'll drive you to my place. You can help me get set up for the party. See? There's no reason you can't come."

"What about my eleven o'clock Friday night curfew?" I said, playing my trump card. Surely the guy was not going to want to leave his party, just when it would be cranking into high gear, to drive me home.

"Not a problem, dude. I'll make sure you get home in time for beddy-bye." He clapped me on the back, and that was that.

It was weird that we even became friends. Aside from both of us going to the same high school, both being sixteen, and both swinging boy parts, we didn't really have that much in common. We're sort of from opposite ends of the social spectrum. Liam's this WASP kid who drives his own car—an electric blue Camaro—thanks to his mom and dad, who are both corporate attorneys. He looks exactly like his dad, only younger, with fine brown hair that he wears in a short cut, a nice face—girls are always telling him he's cute—and a nice bod. He's average height, about five ten, but he's pretty good at sports. Actually, he was on both the baseball and the basketball teams at school, but the coach kicked him off for screwing up. Liam screws up a lot. That's how he got expelled from two private academies and wound up at the public school I attend, East High, in Memphis. Even after getting booted off sports teams and expelled from those fancy academies, Liam was still Mr. Popular when he got to my school.

I'm Mr. Average, Mexican by heritage, brown-skinned with long, curly black hair. My real mother was a teenager, in the US illegally, and she gave me up for adoption before she was deported. That's all I know about her, which is a lot more than I know about my real dad. I love my adoptive mom and dad, Christine and Edmond Stephens. Mom is an elementary school teacher and Dad is a bus driver, so they don't have the money to put me in my own sports car or any private academy. They both say they regret naming me Dale, that they should have named me Jesus or Gomez, something closer to my heritage. I grew up in a white neighborhood with mostly white friends. As I got older and browner, my parents started trying to drop more of my birth culture on me. Dad, who does most of the cooking, made sure we had at least one Mexican dish at every meal. One of Mom's college friends became a Spanish teacher, so Mom got this friend to teach her some Spanish, which she then taught to Dad and me.

Those lessons didn't do me one bit of good when I met a couple of Mexican kids last year. We didn't connect at all. They were stunned and amused that I couldn't follow or respond to the stream of Spanish they shot at me. They were actually better at English than I was at my native tongue. It turns out there are regional differences in pronunciation and vocabulary when it comes to Spanish. The language as spoken in Mexico is not quite the same as that spoken in Cuba, which is not quite the same as that spoken in Spain. Those Mexican kids pointed out that what little Spanish I'd learned was closer to that spoken in Puerto Rico. They also pointed out that I had an "Anglo" accent and said what I spoke was American Spanish. Which, I guess, they didn't consider to be "real" Spanish.

So I'm okay at sports and I'm okay-looking, but I don't have anywhere near the kind of outgoing personality Liam has. I'm the kind of guy who hangs around in the background. But after he got to East High, Liam noticed me for some reason, and we started up a friendship.

WHEN WE got to his house after school on Friday, I was glad to help him get everything together for the party. He downloaded all the music on his phone into the house's sound system and dug an extra set of speakers out of his closet, which I plugged in and set out in the backyard. We placed extra chairs on the deck around the pool and put the cans of beer on ice in big plastic tubs on the patio. Then we hauled card tables down from the attic and set them up on the patio between the plastic tubs. Liam was upbeat and joking around, like always, while we were doing all this. But when we started bringing out big plastic bowls and bags of pretzels and other snacks to set up on the tables, he got very quiet. His smile faded, and he suddenly looked strange, sort of distant. He seemed lost, maybe, or afraid. It was hard to figure exactly what was going through his head, but I could tell it wasn't anything good.

"Hey, what's wrong, man?" I asked.

Liam gave me a distracted look. "Huh?"

"Just now, you looked sorta funny. Are you okay? Is something wrong?"

"No, not at all, dude," he said really fast.

"You sure you want to do this party?"

"Hell yeah! Come on and help me bring out the liquor." He grinned, his eyes brightening as he waved for me to follow him back into the house.

BY TEN o'clock, the party was going strong. I sat under a tree at the edge of the backyard, my back against the trunk, sipping from a can of Diet Pepsi while I watched the happenings. A lot of the kids were already drunk or high. A few guys and gals had stripped down to their underwear and were swimming in the pool. One dude shoved a couple of people into the pool fully clothed. Other kids were dancing on the deck to the loud, throbbing music. Chips and pretzels flew back and forth in a brief food fight. With all the shouting and laughter, things were pretty noisy.

These kids were from rich families, and most of them attended those private academies Liam had gotten himself kicked out of. There wasn't another brown face in sight. I felt out of place. With my curfew closing in, I was getting even more anxious, so I decided it was time for me to take off.

I got up and made my way across the littered lawn and into the house, looking for Liam. Kids were in the kitchen, the hall, and the bedrooms, many of them coupled up and going at each other. I slid past them pretty much unnoticed. I figured Liam was doing the make-out thing in his room, but when I looked in there, I saw some other guy getting his freak on with a couple of girls. The girls both covered their exposed chests with their hands, and the guy shouted at me to close the fucking door, which I did in a hurry.

I checked the living room, the dining room, the garage, and even the front yard, but still no sight of Liam. The only other place was his father's office, but I didn't think Liam would be in there because his dad made it pretty clear that room was off-limits. As I approached the office, I could hear soft moans coming from inside. I knocked and listened for a response, only there was no answer, just more moaning. So I said quietly, "Liam? You in there?"

A FEW seconds passed before I heard his voice. "Dale, come on in."

I opened the door and walked in. There were no lights on. At first I didn't see anyone. Then Liam raised his head up from behind the desk. His shoulders and chest were bare. From the way he looked at me, it was obvious he was hammered, either from booze or bud. "Hey, man," he whispered, his expression empty.

"It's getting late, dude," I said. "I should be hauling my ass home."

"In a minute," he replied. He waved me over. "Come here. Got a present for ya."

I hesitated, my hand still on the doorknob. "Liam, I really need to get out of here."

Someone else sat up then and peered at me over the desk. Alice Chipley. She was on the girls' soccer team at school, a tall, slender, gorgeous blonde who'd been flirting with Liam for about a week now. Her eyes were half-closed as she smiled at me, but it was clear she wasn't drunk. "Hi, Dale," she said. "Don't you want to play with us?"

My heart jumped around in my chest, and suddenly I wanted to just walk away. I stood there for a few more seconds, looking from Alice to Liam, before turning to leave.

"Hey, wait," Liam said, his voice coming out slow and lazy. He grinned at me. "I'll take you home in a minute. Come on, man. Alice thinks you're cute. Don't you think he's cute, Alice?"

She winked at me. "Oh yeah. For sure." She sat up higher, and I could see that she was stripped down to her bra and panties. "Close the door, Dale, and come over here."

Things got really strange. The door seemed to close by itself. Then I found myself on the other side of the room without a clue as to how or when I got there. Alice and Liam were both in their underwear and I was between them. Alice was kissing me, kissing in this teasing, hungry way. Their hands rubbed over my chest, up and down my thighs, squeezing. I couldn't tell Alice's hands from Liam's because those hands seemed to be everywhere at once, and my eyes were closed.

There was a sudden loud clatter and I jerked, my eyes popping open. I saw that Liam had swept everything off his father's desk with one big swipe of his arm. Alice took me by the shoulders and pushed me back onto the desk. She climbed over me and started kissing me again. Liam came up behind her, his face buried in her hair as he nibbled at her ear. I could smell the booze on his breath. Then Alice moved herself to one side, and she took Liam gently by the ear, and she pulled his head down to make him kiss me.

It's hard for me to say exactly how I felt about all this. I wasn't excited at all. I was scared but didn't know why. Alice was a beautiful girl with a great body. Liam was a good-looking guy with a great body. Something about being there with the two of them should have gotten to me and made me want more. I didn't protest or tell them to stop, but I didn't kiss either of them back or touch them. I just sort of let them do what they wanted. At school, I saw guys and girls flirt with each other all the time, saw the attraction that other kids felt. I knew I should have been feeling the things they felt, doing the things they did. Only I didn't. I was sixteen years old, sixteen freaking years old, and even with two of the hottest kids in school all over me, I just felt nothing. I didn't know what I wanted. I didn't know where I belonged. I didn't know where I fit in my own life.

Alice unbuttoned my shirt. Liam fumbled drunkenly with the button and zipper on my jeans. I closed my eyes and wished I was someone else, somewhere else.

I don't know how long I was in the office with Liam and Alice, but at some point, the party went completely dead. The music stopped, along with all the shouting and laughing. I didn't notice that until the door opened and the light went on in the office. Alice, Liam, and I looked at the door and saw Liam's dad standing there. The four of us were frozen in place for about a minute. Then Mr. Mason got this look of absolute rage on his face. Liam stood straight up at that, looking as if he was about to beg for mercy, but he turned instead and puked all over the stuff he'd knocked off the desk.

LIAM WAS too wasted to drive, so his dad called my parents and my mom came to pick me up. My mom and dad were upset that I not only missed curfew but was at an unsupervised party where there were alcohol and drugs. That got me grounded for a month, but judging from the way Mr. Mason cursed at him, I figured Liam was in for even worse punishment.

Liam didn't show up at school Tuesday after the Labor Day break. He didn't show up Wednesday or Thursday either. I tried calling him, but his cell phone had been turned off, and when I asked Alice, she said she hadn't heard from him either. Friday I came to school early for choral practice, and when I went to my locker, I saw Liam alone in the hall. He was clearing stuff out of his own locker, shoving it into a backpack.

He wouldn't look at me when I walked up to him. He just kept on unloading his locker. "Hey, Liam," I said. "I was worried about you. Are you okay, man?"

He shrugged, still not looking at me.

"That was so weird, your dad showing up when he did."

"Not really," Liam replied. "Mr. Scopes next door got pissed about all the noise. But instead of calling the cops, he called my dad."

"Oh." I paused, not sure what to say next. "Well, it's good the neighbor didn't call the cops, huh? Somebody would've gotten arrested for sure."

"Yeah, I guess." His voice was so down and lifeless.

That scared me. "Liam? Are you all right? What happened with your dad?"

Liam shrugged again. "He's kicking me out. He says he wants me out of the house."

"What? Are you kidding me?"

"He says I could have gotten him and my mom arrested or sued with all those underage kids drinking and doing drugs at the house. He says I'll never be anything but a fuck-up. Maybe he's right. Anyway, I'm leaving, man. My mom is sending me down to my Uncle James in El Paso. I'll finish school there."

"When are you leaving?"

"I'm booked on a flight this afternoon." He shut the locker, zipped up his backpack, and finally looked at me. There was real affection in his eyes. He leaned over and kissed me on the mouth. "You really are cute, Dale. I'll be in touch."

He gave me that crooked smile and left. I stood there, staring after him, and it was only after the door swung shut behind him that I realized how much I did not want him to leave.

GENE GANT grew up in Memphis, Tennessee, and lives with his family in a quiet little rural community just outside the city.

Faking Truth

JO RAMSEY

MY FIRST day of high school, I saw a guy in the cafeteria before first period wearing nail polish and a women's scarf around his neck. He had short hair, and other than the nail polish and scarf, his clothes looked pretty guyish. But he still gave me hope. If he could come to school dressed like that, maybe I'd be able to be myself too. I couldn't at home, but my parents wouldn't know what I did at school unless I caused enough trouble for someone to call them.

The next time I saw the nail polish boy, between my second and third classes, three guys in football jerseys were bouncing him off a locker. So much for hope.

That first day, every teacher I had took attendance. I cringed when each of them said, "Jacob Landry." That was the name on my birth certificate, which meant it was the one the school knew. But it wasn't a name that felt right to me. It never had.

My parents could have given me a unisex name. Something like Robin or Avery or Hunter or something. But no. They'd stuck me with Jacob. A name that was obviously for the boy they'd assumed I was when the doctor told them I had a penis. The boy I wasn't but had no choice other than to pretend to be.

Every time a teacher called that name, though, I answered. I didn't have a choice about that either. They would have marked me absent otherwise, which would have caused problems. Either that or one of my classmates, all of whom had known me pretty much since kindergarten, would have ratted me out.

By the time lunch rolled around, I felt so sick to my stomach I didn't know if I'd even be able to stand the smell of the school food, let alone actually eat it. I wasn't a liar. My whole life, my brother and sister had teased me about how honest I was. At least, they'd teased me when they weren't ticked off at me for telling Mom and Dad about something they'd done. My parents were usually amused by the honesty thing too, unless they forgot to tell me to keep quiet about something.

Or unless I said something they didn't want to hear, like the time when I was five. They caught me in my sister's room wearing her outgrown fairy princess costume, waving a wand over a group of dolls. When they asked why I was dressed and playing that way, I said, "Lola says this is what girls do, and I'm a girl."

They dragged me to the doctor and to a shrink, both of whom told them it was probably just a stage and they should let me explore it but also encourage me to dress and play like a boy. I didn't try telling the doctor and psychiatrist that I wasn't a boy. I was afraid they would stick me in a hospital and not let me out until I was fixed.

After that, the only thing I wasn't honest about was myself. And every time I went through the motions of being a boy, I hated myself a little bit more.

That was why I wanted to heave my guts out when I walked into the cafeteria. The combination of noise, smells, and heat was more than I could stand. I didn't even make it halfway to the line before I realized I had to get out of there before I blacked out. Fainting in front of over a hundred high school students on the first day of school would definitely not have been a good idea.

I didn't make it out of the cafeteria, though. A teacher I hadn't seen before stepped in front of me. She was a few inches taller than me and about twice as wide, and there was no chance of getting around her. She didn't exactly look scary, but something about her definitely told me not to push my luck.

"Are you a ninth grader?" she asked.

I gulped and nodded. I couldn't make myself actually speak.

"In case you missed the rules, you aren't allowed to leave the cafeteria during your lunch period." She paused. "It is your lunch period, yes? You aren't here by mistake?"

"No. I mean yes." She couldn't possibly have made her questions any more confusing.

She smiled, which took away some of the intimidation factor. "I'm assuming you mean this is your lunch period. I'm Mrs. Graylock. I'm the librarian."

"I'm…." I stopped myself. My parents had brought me up to show proper manners. Shaking hands, introducing myself if someone else didn't introduce me, all that stuff. I had to introduce myself to Mrs. Graylock, because she didn't have any other way to know who I was, but I didn't want to say my birth name. I wanted to be my true self.

Of course, that wasn't possible, so I swallowed and said, "I'm Jacob Landry."

"It's nice to meet you." Mrs. Graylock looked around. "Do you have friends in here who you can sit with? I know it's a little overwhelming, but I can't let you walk out."

"Probably." I didn't really have any friends at all. In kindergarten and first grade, I'd wanted to play with the other girls. That was okay when I was five and six, but once I got older than that, boys were supposed to play with boys. I couldn't keep playing with the girls when I couldn't tell anyone I was one. So I'd stopped playing with anyone at all.

By now, people talked to me at school or if they saw me around town, but that was it. They weren't exactly mean. I sometimes heard them say I was weird or a snob. No other insults, though, at least not where I could hear. They didn't really say much at all.

Probably someone would let me sit at their table. They would ignore me, but at least I wouldn't be standing in the middle of the room about to fall over because the librarian wouldn't let me out.

"Are you all right?" Mrs. Graylock's smile faded, and she looked concerned. "You're really pale. Come sit down over here. I'll have someone get your lunch if you want, or I'll tell the worker to hold something for you until you're able to get it."

"I'm fine." I glanced around. No one *seemed* to be paying attention to us, but that didn't mean they weren't. "I'll just get something and find a seat."

She tilted her head. "Listen," she said so quietly I almost didn't hear her. "I'm not supposed to tell you or anyone else this. And I'm not supposed to do it, so I'd really prefer you not pass it along. But during lunch, I leave the library open in case anyone needs a safe place. You're in here now, so I have to keep you in here. But just for future reference."

I nodded, and for the first time all day, something that felt kind of like a smile curved my lips. I wouldn't have to be in the cafeteria from now on, as long as no one found out where I was going. That sounded like a pretty good deal to me.

"If you're sure you're okay, go ahead and buy your lunch," she said. "If you need help finding a place to sit, just let me know. But don't take too long, or you won't have time to eat."

"Thanks." I didn't know what else to say, so I just walked away.

I bought a lunch I didn't want and sat with some kids I knew well enough to say hi to. As I'd figured, they mostly ignored me, so I returned the favor. I didn't actually eat anything, just poked at the food until it was time to leave.

The rest of the day was the same as the first part. Before lunch, I'd had three classes. After lunch, I only had two, and then the day was over. I was proud of myself for surviving the first day of high school, but that was overshadowed by hating the fact that I still had to be Jacob.

I didn't want to walk home with the other five hundred and something kids. The people in my grade would leave me alone, but some of the older kids made me nervous. Like the football players who'd slammed nail polish boy into the lockers.

Instead of leaving like everyone else, I decided to go check out the library. Maybe Mrs. Graylock would let me hang out for a little while, if she wasn't one of the teachers who left right after school.

She was still at her desk, and a couple of girls were chatting with her. I hesitated at the door. I didn't know the girls, and I didn't want to intrude. But I also didn't want to just stand outside like an idiot, so I went in.

"Hi, Jacob." Mrs. Graylock smiled. "This is Hayley and Nia. We were just talking about books and movies, and which are better."

"Oh." I didn't know if she expected me to say anything about the topic, so I kept quiet.

"We have to go," Hayley said. "Soccer practice. Go see that movie, Mrs. Graylock. I think you'll like it better than the book."

"I'm a librarian. I can't like movies better than books." Mrs. Graylock grinned. "Have a good practice, girls. See you tomorrow."

The girls left. I was a lot more comfortable without them there, though I didn't want to say so.

"So how was the first day of high school?" Mrs. Graylock asked. "You look much better than you did at lunch."

"I got through it," I said.

"That doesn't sound very positive."

I didn't know what to say. I ran into that problem a lot. If I talked, I had to talk like Jacob, which meant having to try to think like a boy. That just didn't work for me. And I was too scared of anyone finding out who I was and telling my parents, so it was safer to just be quiet.

Even though Mrs. Graylock had seemed kind of scary at first in the cafeteria, though, she had something else about her. I didn't know what to call it, but it made me feel safe. She'd said she left the library open for people who needed a safe place to be during lunch. Maybe she was a safe person to talk to.

I couldn't be my true self to everyone. Not yet. Probably not until I was eighteen, and maybe not even then. But if I had one person at school who knew who I really was, maybe things would be a little easier. I didn't have any reason to trust Mrs. Graylock, but it wouldn't hurt to try.

I went closer to the counter. "If I tell you something, do you have to tell anyone else, or can it just be between us?"

She wrinkled her forehead. "That depends on what you tell me. If it's about someone being hurt or in danger, then yes, I do have to tell someone. Otherwise, I can try to keep it to myself unless I think someone needs help."

"No one's getting hurt or anything." I paused. Maybe this wasn't such a great idea. But I was ready to start letting my true self show. I was tired of faking the truth. I wanted someone to know what it really was. "Um, okay. Just please don't tell anyone, or at least tell me if you're going to."

"I promise that if I have to tell someone, I will let you know first." She leaned over the counter.

She was close enough for me to whisper, so I did. "My name is Jacob, and everyone sees me as a boy, but I'm not. I'm a girl. I just can't really be one."

Mrs. Graylock's eyes widened, and she didn't say anything. That scared me. I'd taken a huge chance, and I'd probably really screwed up. And I couldn't take it back.

But after a minute or so, she nodded slowly and smiled. "I'm really honored that you trusted me enough to tell me that. And it is something I can keep between us. Your parents don't know?"

"They know I'm a girl." I shook my head. "I mean, when I was little, I told them I was a girl. They kind of freaked out, so ever since, I've been trying to act like a boy so they won't be upset."

"That's very brave and very considerate of you." She hesitated. "I'm sorry your parents aren't able to accept who you are. I've known other kids who were somewhere along the gender spectrum other than what matched their anatomy. Some had supportive parents, some didn't."

"There's a gender spectrum?" That didn't make a lot of sense to me. I'd seen things online about being genderfluid or genderqueer or things like that, but I didn't totally understand them. I'd been taught there were males and females, and that was all. Obviously I had a few things to learn.

Mrs. Graylock nodded. "There is, and I have some books about gender identity that I can loan you if you'd like. It might be better if you read them here, though."

"Maybe."

"So what is your name?"

I blinked a few times. I'd told her my name already. She'd used it more than once. "What do you mean?"

"Jacob is a boy's name, and you just told me you aren't a boy." She stood up. "So what is your name? I'd like to call you something that makes you comfortable and happy, at least when we're talking alone like this."

"I don't know." I hadn't given much thought about what I wanted my name to be. I'd never figured I would actually be allowed to be a girl until I grew up, and I'd planned to choose a new name then. There didn't seem to be much point in picking out a name I wouldn't have been able to use.

But now, I might be able to use a new name. At least when I visited the school library. And maybe giving myself a name I liked would help me feel better about being a girl, even if my parents didn't like the idea.

Mrs. Graylock didn't say anything, but this time I wasn't worried. The way she was looking at me, I figured she was giving me a chance to think.

Then a name popped into my head. The name of the place on Earth I most wanted to visit, and it was also a girl's name. It would be perfect.

"Sydney," I said.

Mrs. Graylock nodded again. "It's nice to meet you, Sydney."

That name in someone else's voice sounded even more perfect. And I knew I'd made the right choice, both with the name and by trusting Mrs. Graylock.

I still had to fake the truth for everyone else, but at least I had one person who would let me be myself. And that was a start.

JO RAMSEY is a former special education teacher who now writes full time. She firmly believes that everyone has it in them to be a hero, whether to others or in their own lives, and she tries to write books that encourage teens to be themselves and make a difference. Jo has been writing since age five and has been writing young adult fiction since she was a teen herself; her first YA book was published in 2010. She lives in Massachusetts with her two daughters, her husband, and two cats, one of whom likes to read over her shoulder.

Website: http://www.joramsey.com

Facebook: https://www.facebook.com/JoRamseyYA

Twitter: @JoRamseyYA

Tumblr: http://joramseyya.tumblr.com

Eric's Secret

SAM KADENCE

SEEING HIS cousin Marissa in a wheelchair was a little shocking to Eric at first. They'd been inseparable as kids. Practically twins until his folks had moved to California for work. He couldn't imagine anyone hurting her. Now she needed help to walk, someone to support her through rehab, and to encourage her to not let the horrible memory of an abusive boyfriend put her head in the wrong place. He could pretend that was why he was here, but he'd been sent to Minnesota—shipped across the country for his senior year of high school—to cover up his mistakes.

"Hey, Rissa. You're looking great," Eric greeted her as his uncle pulled his bags out of the trunk of the car. He leaned down to hug her. "Mama said you'd be out of the chair by the beginning of the new school year."

Marissa's smile was genuine as she accepted his hug. "How about you? You're a little pale. Don't think I can't tell under that dark skin of yours. You'll have to fill me in. All we've heard is rumors."

Eric sighed. He didn't really want to rehash the past year of his life. "Long story short?"

She shrugged.

"I got a girl pregnant."

Marissa's eyes widened in shock. "But…." She glanced at her dad, who vanished into the house with Eric's stuff. "What about the baby?"

"Her parents made her abort." Eric's heart hurt at the thought. As much pain, fear, and uncertainty as the situation had brought, he had still hoped for a glimpse of the baby. Maybe even a chance to see it grow. He watched his little brothers and sisters run around and wondered if that could have been his baby.

"I'm so sorry."

Eric shrugged and helped Marissa push her chair up the ramp and into the house, greeted her mom, and made his way to his room—the one he'd used whenever he visited before. Here he actually got his own bedroom. He wondered what he'd do with all the solitude.

Marissa wheeled herself into the room. "Doors don't lock anymore. Daddy did that after…." Her words faded off as she seemed to remember the reason, which had to be her ex-boyfriend. "If you ever want to talk, mine is always open. And not just because Mom and Dad say it should be."

"Thanks, Rissa." Eric dropped down onto the bed.

She rolled across to him and tugged on his curly hair. "Bit of a 'fro going on here."

Eric had purposely let it go to make his dad happy. His faded, torn-up jeans and too large T-shirt were for that reason too. Hell, he'd screwed Aria because his dad demanded he get a girlfriend. He was supposed to have felt something for her. An attraction, he guessed—she'd been pretty enough. Surviving high school without dating made him weird, and probably gay, or so the guys at school claimed even though Aria was vocal about their sex lives. But he'd never met anyone, male or female, who interested him like the other kids seemed interested in everyone else. Sex didn't interest him. Being intimate with Aria had been a chore. He'd worked hard to find an emotional connection with her, only all she ever talked about was the newest cell phone or which of her friends was screwing which football player. She had been about as deep as a half can of soda.

"I can help you fix it if you want. My friend Paige has curls—not as tight as yours—but I've gotten good at fixing her hair."

What if he told Marissa? Not just pieces? Everything? She'd hate him too, right? No. She wouldn't understand. Eric gave her a half smile and pulled free from her touch. "I'm good. Just tired from the trip. Maybe I'll take a nap."

"Sure. Four hours on a plane would zap me too. I have some friends from school coming over tonight for a pizza party. Don't hide, okay? I want you to meet them. They're nice."

Eric sighed to himself. He really didn't want to meet anyone. The more people he met, the more not normal he felt.

ERIC'S SECRET | 45

"Get some rest," Marissa said and left him alone.

Eric leaned back in the bed and opened his phone. He had restricted his Facebook page so no one could friend him or post to his wall without his approval. He could only handle so many insults thrown his way. Wasn't bad enough he'd been born a mutt to an Irish mother and an African American father in a state of blue-eyed blonds. He had to be different too.

Marissa's dad had left Eric's bags beside the door. People didn't know Eric here. He could pretend for a while. He was good at pretending, but he was so tired of it.

VOICES WOKE him a little while later. Marissa and another feminine voice. One of the friends, maybe? The smell of pizza wafted through the room. Eric's gut clenched in hunger. He swung out of bed, did a quick armpit sniff to make sure he didn't stink, and then made his way toward the kitchen. He couldn't answer questions if his mouth was full. So all he had to do was keep his face stuffed. *That* was normal guy behavior.

The girl sitting with Marissa in the kitchen made him pause. She was a mass of wild red curls, freckled peach skin, and sparkling skirts. She also had a slight Adam's apple. "Eric, come meet Paige. We work together at that old vintage clothing shop down on Main," Marissa said.

Eric took a seat beside Marissa, eyeing the pizza and her friend. "Hey" was all he said.

"He's cute," Paige told Marissa. Her voice was soft but huskier than Eric expected. "Bet if we ran some product through his hair, he'd have half the school flirting." She pushed the pizza box across the table. "Eat. Dmitri's pizza is legendary. And the boys will be here soon. There won't be anything left if you wait."

Eric opened the box and took a slice of pizza almost as big as his head. Food. Mouth. No speak. Hmm.

"So you're seventeen, right?" Paige asked.

Eric nodded.

"Dating someone?"

Marissa glared at her friend. "Paige."

"He got a girl pregnant. Big deal. Bet he's a firm believer in protection now. I can't get pregnant anyway."

Eric swallowed a groan. The last thing he wanted was another girlfriend. The pressure to conform was too much. He was just another square peg that wouldn't fit into a round world.

"So is she still your girlfriend?"

"No." Aria had just been a cover. They'd barely been friends. He could count on one hand the number of friends he'd had, and since his little disaster with Aria, that number had dropped to zero.

"No girlfriend, then. Boyfriend?"

"No," Eric said firmly. Always the assumption. He guessed it didn't really matter. People always thought what they wanted to. He was a freak. He knew that.

"Just in between for the moment or no interest in either?" Paige asked.

He stared at her. Did she know? Could she tell somehow? Who was this girl?

"Don't mind Paige," Marissa told him. "She's just really nosy."

Paige stuck her tongue out. The doorbell rang. Paige jumped up. "Must be the boys. I'll let them in." She rushed off to the door in a flurry of skirts and swaying hips that Eric couldn't recall ever seeing outside of a movie.

"She?" Eric asked his only question about Marissa's friend.

Marissa nodded. "She. Be nice."

"I'm always nice," Eric insisted and grabbed another slice of pizza. The group who joined them at the table was nothing like he expected. Four guys, one in heels and makeup, two looking athletic, and the fourth a redhead with a box beard. Eric had always wanted a beard like that—it looked so sophisticated—but nothing grew on his face except fuzz.

"Everyone, meet my cousin Eric. Eric, this is Bas, Adam, Ru, and Dane." Heels was Bas; athletic, Adam and Ru; and beard, Dane. "Adam is a senior with us. Ru is his boyfriend. Bas just graduated. He and Dane are a couple."

Great, more romance. Why did he have to exist in a world that insisted love and sex was the norm? Was there any place he'd fit in? "Does that mean you and Paige?" Eric had to ask.

Paige laughed and sat down on the opposite side of him. "I like boys, sweets. M does too, even if we both have the habit of choosing the wrong ones."

"We're screening all their dates now," Ru said.

"Probably for the best," Eric agreed. Did Paige come from some abusive relationship too? Why did people bother when it caused so much pain?

Adam pulled out a MacBook Air and flipped it open. "So we have a couple weeks to put together the details needed for our GSA. We need space, a teacher or parent to supervise, a goal that doesn't make kids groan about showing up, and money to fund things like publicity and field trips."

Eric hoped he wouldn't offend Marissa's friends the first night he was in town. It would make for a miserable year. She'd always had good grades and he only did so-so. "GSA?" he asked.

"Gay-Straight Alliance," Marissa answered. "A group to get straight and gay people together to talk about issues and show support to each other."

Rainbows, hearts, and all that bullshit. Boxes, labels, and stigmas that he would never fit into. Whatever. Eric pushed away from the table. "I'll let you get to it, then."

"Stay," Paige said, putting her hand on his arm. "The more the merrier."

"Pretty sure I don't fit in your group," Eric told her.

She glanced around the room. "You're standing in a room with three gay boys, one bi boy, a straight girl, and a transgender one. There is no not fitting into this group."

"Mhmm." Eric shrugged off her touch. She had no idea. He leaned over to kiss Marissa's cheek—"Later, Rissa"—and headed for his room. He would never fit into a group that was all about sex when he had no interest in it, not the gender, the act, or even the concept. He longed for a connection. Someone to talk to who understood him and could share things with him, but none of that was related to his body. Looks that made other boys embarrassed didn't do things to him. And that made him a freak.

He dug out his book reader and opened the latest adventure novel. It was all so easy in the books and movies. One look across the room could mean instant love and an unbreakable connection. That's what Eric wanted but was pretty sure he was never going to find.

He was halfway through the book when a quiet knock on the door jarred him out of the alternate world. It was the heels guy, Bas.

"Hey, we're gonna go get some ice cream. Marissa was hoping you'd come. I promise there will be no talk of the GSA over ice cream, just sugar and laughter. Nelson's has cones that never end and something like eighty different flavors," Bas told him.

Eric thought about what he had left of his cash. He could probably afford an ice cream. He'd have to find a job here soon but had enough to last a few weeks if he was careful. "Sure."

Bas nodded and left. Eric got up and glanced at his clothes. Maybe he should change. Looking like he just rolled out of bed was okay for hanging around the house. Not so much for being seen in public with Marissa's very perfect friends. He changed into a pair of better-fitting jeans and a short-sleeve button-up, then ran some product through his hair to relieve some of the frizz. When he stepped into the living room, Paige whistled.

"Cleans up well," she said.

Bas reached out and squeezed Eric's hand. "You ready? We're taking the Corbins' SUV." He pointed at Adam. "Should be room for all of us."

"Ready as I'm going to be." Eric followed them out to the vehicle and helped Marissa in, then loaded her chair in the back before climbing in himself. Adam drove and everyone talked—Dane about some recipe he was working on, Ru about an upcoming show, and Paige about some outfit she'd found at the vintage shop. Eric just listened.

They parked on the street, and Eric helped Marissa back into her chair before they made their way to the shop. The line was long, and there was no place to sit inside, but outside in the warm sunshine there was a mass of tables. He watched people walk away from the counter with giant cones heaping with enormous scoops of ice cream. "Holy crap," he said.

"Birthday cake is my favorite flavor. Though caramel vanilla cone is a pretty close second," Marissa told him. Paige took the chair from him and leaned over to chat with Marissa.

Both sounded good. Eric stared at the list of flavors as they waited. He wasn't a big sweets fan but could eat ice cream with the best of them.

"First time?"

Eric glanced up and met the warm brown eyes of a Hispanic guy in line behind them.

"It's intimidating at first. Lots to try. Huge cones."

Eric nodded. "First time. Not much on sweets."

The guy held out his hand. "Luis."

"Eric." He took Luis's hand and shook it.

"What sort of flavors you like?"

"Something not as sweet?" Eric replied.

Luis smiled. "They have a tart flavor that I'd bet you'd like. Add a scoop of something sweet in the middle and the rest tart. I'm not much for sweet either."

"Sounds good," Eric said, choosing the birthday cake as his scoop of sweet flavor. He noticed the sign that said they were hiring. "I wonder if you have to be eighteen to work here."

"Nah. Sixteen. But it's summer only. Gets cold in the winter here. No one much buys ice cream then." Luis followed as the line began to shuffle forward. "Lines are always like this in the summer, though. Your arms get tired of scooping all the time."

"You work here?"

"Last summer. Now I work at the grocery store. More hours, not as fun. But that's life, eh?"

Eric nodded. That was for sure.

"If you're looking for something longer, the grocery store is hiring. You a Northern kid?"

It seemed an odd question, but Eric knew his new high school was called Northern. "Yeah. Senior year."

"Just graduated myself. Going to the community college next to the high school now. And working. You not from here?"

"California."

"Ah. Sunshine. You'll miss that in January."

"Is it really that bad?"

Luis shrugged. "Can be. You like to ice skate or ski or something?"

Eric shook his head.

"Ah, then yeah. That bad."

They finally reached the counter. Eric ordered his ice cream. Luis ordered the same. The girls had birthday cake ice cream with something that looked chocolate. The guys were too far ahead for Eric to hear them. He paid for his cone and followed everyone to the table. He glanced back at Luis, who seemed to be alone, and decided to take a stab in the dark at making a friend. "Want to join us?" Eric asked as Luis left the counter with his cone.

He glanced at their table and nodded. "Sure."

Eric introduced Luis around, and everyone ate and talked. Adam was still talking about the GSA thing. It annoyed Eric, mostly because it seemed like one more closed door.

"Important to include the whole spectrum," Luis said to Adam.

"Lesbian, gay, straight, trans. Everyone's welcome."

"Asexual? Pansexual? More labels if you need them. Not everyone is attracted to a gender. Myself, I like people. Sex, eh." Luis shrugged. "Could take it or leave it. Gotta know the person, be real with them. Doesn't matter what's between their legs. It's what's between their eyes that turns me on."

Eric blinked at Luis, a bit of shock rolling through him. Was there really someone out there like him? Was he really not a freak?

"I never thought about that," Adam said. "They were just sort of letters in an acronym."

"We're all like that till we know someone who is one of those letters. Why do you think some of those straight people are so crazy about not wanting gays around? No diversity. The community college has a group with a couple of psych students running it. We have all shades in the group. Thought I was a freak until a girl stepped out and described it." Luis licked his ice cream. "Not a freak. Just looking for love with my brain first. So it takes a little longer."

Eric let the words process. Not a freak. Love was still an option? Even if he didn't care for sex? "Can I come to the college group?" he asked Luis.

"Sure. It's open to anyone. We have some as young as fifteen." He glanced at Adam. "Maybe you want to visit so you can better plan your group?"

Adam nodded. "Maybe I should."

"There are more like us?" Eric had to ask. "Asexual?" No one gasped or shrieked at him when he admitted it. Without the Internet, he never would have known what he was, but he'd met enough trolls on it not to want to engage with most of the sites out there.

"You are not alone. You don't have to be alone."

"Be what you are. Not what the world wants you to be," Bas told Eric.

Eric smiled. There was hope after all. He felt like the weight had been lifted off his shoulders. And maybe, just maybe, he didn't have to pretend anymore.

SAM KADENCE has always dreamed about being someone else, somewhere else. With very little musical talent, Sam decided the only way to make those dreams come true was to try everything from cosplay at the local anime conventions to writing novels about pretending to run away to become a musician.

Sam has a bachelor's degree in Creative Writing, sells textbooks for a living, enjoys taking photographs of Asian Ball Joint Dolls to tell more stories, and has eclectic taste in music from J-pop to rock and country. All of which finds its way into the books eventually.

Facebook: https://www.facebook.com/SamKadence

The Most Beautiful Boy in the Whole World

AMY LANE

"KIERNAN—'SUP?"

Kiernan smiled tentatively at Dean Argus, the guy who helped his dad in the garage. Dean had lush pillow lips and a chiseled chin and stunning green eyes—it was hard not to stare. His skin was pale gold, even around his upper arms and chest, and barely a hint of freckles remained under his eyes and across his nose. He was, quite simply, the most beautiful boy in the world.

"Uhm, nothin'. Is my sister around?"

"Chelsea?" One corner of Dean's lush mouth lifted, and he wiped his hands determinedly with a cloth, like Chelsea was a reason to get cleaner. "Naw. She's got practice or something like that. Why?"

Kiernan shook his head. "No reason. Selby's coming by. He, uhm, likes my sister."

Dean grimaced. "Selby needs to keep his likes to himself," he said shortly, and Kiernan shrugged. Yeah, well, so Dean liked Chelsea too. Shocker. Chelsea was almost seventeen and Dean was almost twenty—made sense, right?

Well, yeah, to everybody but Kiernan and Selby.

Selby peeked his head around the corner of the garage just when Dean shoved his head back under the hood of the car. "Kier?"

"Yeah—coming!" Kiernan eyed his backpack on the truck bench seat near the back of the auto bay and decided he'd leave it there. He and Selby were probably just going to hang out at the creek anyway—he didn't want to risk his books. "Uh, bye, Dean. Uh, see you tomorrow, 'kay? Tell Chelsea we were here, 'kay?" *Shoot me now, 'kay?*

Dean smiled, and Kiernan may have been thirteen, but he recognized the pity in the smile. Oh, who the hell was he kidding? Chelsea must have told him—they flirted together most days after school. Kiernan had attended his first GSA meeting in the seventh grade and come out to his family.

Nobody had been surprised.

So everybody was out now, and that was happy fine, except Kiernan's sister felt entitled to tell everybody how cute her gay little brother was, and now Kiernan's crush on the straight guy his dad had hired was public knowledge.

Awesome.

Kiernan made his way out of the garage, careful not to knock anything over with his suddenly out-of-control elbows. His dad told him every year, "Let me know if you want to work in the garage, son!" but Kiernan could read the hint of panic in Eddie Brennan's eyes. His father got the whole gay thing, was not freaked out about Kiernan eventually bringing home a boyfriend, and Kiernan believed him when he said that he'd never, ever wished for a straight son, not once. But nobody wanted a four-star spazzmonkey like Kiernan around heavy machinery, especially at the tail end of a growth spurt that had him nearing five foot nine with no signs of slowing down.

His feet were a size fourteen already.

Selby'd once said that his big fear was that Kiernan would stick his head under the hood of a car and then sprout up a foot while he was working on it. They'd laughed for half an hour, but Kiernan hadn't been able to explain the visual on that one to anybody else since.

"She there?" Selby said hopefully as Kiernan walked into the bright autumn sunshine of their small town.

Kiernan shook his head. "No, man—something about cheerleading practice. I, uhm,"—oh, Kiernan didn't want to be the bearer of bad news—"I think Dean was lying, honestly. I sort of think she was there and hiding from us."

He watched Selby anxiously, worried that his crush on Kiernan's sister would come crashing into the dust in an apocalypse of pain.

He should have known better.

Selby had straight brown hair that often fell into his eyes and a lot of freckles across his nose. He said sometimes that he grew his hair long to hide his freckles, but Kiernan knew that was bullshit. He grew his hair long because he knew it looked good when he gave his head a little shake to get it out of his eyes.

That's what he did now, and followed it up with a catlike smile from his wide and generous mouth.

"Classic!" he said, covering his eyes and shaking his head again. "Just freaking classic! Oh my God! This right here is why I should have had a crush on Dean instead!"

Kiernan glared at him sharply. "Because Dean's probably banging my sister?" Selby said things like that all the time—like if he was gay, he and Kiernan would have more to talk about, which was stupid. When they were in second grade, they could go on and on about homophones. Now in the eighth grade, they could go on and on about monkeys in space. Selby had always known Kiernan liked boys—but since Selby showed interest in girls, Kiernan had staunchly kept himself from having wedding fantasies about his best friend.

"No," Selby snorted. "Because he's *hot*!"

Now see? There it was. Normally Kiernan could just let that pass, but the thought that Dean was back in the garage, probably kissing Kiernan's sister, stung just enough to make Kiernan say something. Kiernan glared at him as they turned right off the town's main drag and down one of the smaller residential streets. They were going to the park to play in the creek, like they did every Friday after school when it was sunny. That was their place.

"You know, you don't have to do that."

"Do what?"

"Talk about boys like you think they're hot."

"But I *do* think they're hot!" Selby said it with a manic expression and lots of nodding, and Kiernan was pretty sure he wasn't trying to be taken seriously.

"It's not funny to pretend you're gay!" Kiernan said, feeling angry, like somehow Selby was making fun of *him*.

"I'm not pretending!" Selby responded, and the playfulness had dropped from his voice.

Kiernan glared at him in the gold light filtering through the green leaves and dust of their little town. Suddenly, without warning, the idea that Selby could be gay too hurt him enough that he couldn't speak. He stood there, flailing his hands, thinking about all the times they'd lain on the floor, poring over a fantasy magazine or a film memorabilia catalog. Selby had been… been… *that close,* when Dean had been twenty years old and a million miles away.

"What?" Selby asked, his eyes bright and shiny with hurt.

A car passed them, going fast, and they both took a step into the yard they were standing by, in the shadow of the fruitless mulberry tree that graced the yard.

"Seriously?" Kiernan asked. "You… you never told me."

Selby shrugged. "My folks… you know. You come home, say you're gay, your dad and your sister say that's great. My folks… just as easy to have a crush on a girl, I guess."

Kiernan swallowed. "Do you really?"

"Really what?"

"Think girls are attractive?"

Selby shrugged. "Just like boys, I guess." He tried for a smile, but it was only a shade of his usual grin. "Both good for the baby boner, right?"

They'd measured in the sixth grade, before Kiernan had come out even to himself. It had been reassuring to think they'd grow.

"Not me," Kiernan whispered.

Selby nodded, looked away. "I know not you. Thought… you know. You could like boys, I could girls—it would be our thing, right?"

Kiernan blinked hard against the burn in his eyes. "But… but… why couldn't you like *me?*"

Selby's jaw dropped, his expression so shocked that Kiernan's hurt bloomed, took over his body, and walking down to the creek to play with minnows was suddenly as far out of the realm of possibility as the moon.

"Never mind," Kiernan mumbled, too devastated to even pretend. "I gotta…. I forgot my backpack. See you tomorrow. Bye—"

And he took off running for the haven of the garage, praying Selby wouldn't follow, too destroyed to even see if he would try.

His sneakers crunched on the gravel as he neared the closed bay door, and if he'd been thinking, he would have wondered why Dean closed it. Usually it stood open, but nothing mattered. Kiernan opened the door to the office and then the door to the garage, his heart beating too loudly in his own ears to hear Selby coming up behind him—

Or hear the noises coming from the couch in the garage.

So when he opened the door, he was shocked to see Dean standing naked from the waist down, stroking his erection, while Chelsea knelt on the couch in front of him. She was staring at Dean with a look of utter devotion, and Kiernan—who was used to seeing his sister running around in her underwear and a bra—didn't even register that she wasn't dressed much either.

Until Selby burst in behind him and breathed "Nice tits!" in Kiernan's ear.

Their gazes met in a horrified, laughing collision that left no room for awkwardness or regret or recent revelations.

Their crushes were banging each other, and they'd seen it, and the only people in the entire *world* who would understand were Kiernan and Selby, who had always been together.

Kiernan quietly shut the garage door, and then, as though driven by the same motor, they both ran helter-skelter out of the garage office and back toward the creek. Kiernan stretched his legs and breathed evenly, like he did on the track when they had to run the mile, and he knew Selby was right behind him, his own long legs making light work of the run.

Oh God, it felt good, breathing in the cool edge of autumn, running until the sweat ran under his T-shirt and the waistband of his jeans. They ran past the few shops, past the houses, deep into the shadows of their little Northern California town, where the "wedding park" sat, quiet, cool, shrouded by shadows, and twinkling with the music of the water moving through the center.

Kiernan aimed for the bank of the stream and stumbled to a halt. He rested his hands on his knees and let his breathing overtake him for a moment, his brain happy and clear of all the muddle of people and hurt and crushes.

Running was still a beautiful thing, like when he and Selby were kids and they could race for the sheer joy of moving their bodies.

Selby panted next to him, hands on his hips, stretching his chest out as he turned his face to the sun-dappled shade.

"We need to join track next year," he said, and Kiernan had his first thought about what their life would be like in high school.

They'd need each other.

"Yeah," he breathed, glad he could find the wind to talk. "That can be our thing."

"I'm sorry," Selby said next, and some of Kiernan's earlier hurt fought against the tightness in his chest.

"For what?"

"For making it a joke. I didn't know how to tell you."

Kiernan sighed. "Yeah. Well. I mean, you didn't want me crushing on you, right? Because who wants someone crushing on you when you're still looking around, and you can look anywhere, right?"

He pulled in a big gulp of air then, because it was a long sentence, and Selby just shook his head.

"Don't be a dick," he muttered.

Kiernan kicked sand at him, and Selby kicked back for a minute, and then they were wrestling, like they'd always wrestled, even when Kiernan had come out. Kiernan thought that maybe it just hadn't settled in yet, that Selby would figure out eventually that Kiernan could get turned on by his body, and they'd stop.

But it turned out that Selby probably knew the difference too. There was a difference in the way you touched people. When you were wrestling around, it usually stayed wrestling, unless….

Unless Kiernan noticed that Selby's hair was red in the golden light, and that his lips were a sort of rust-tinted pink, and plump.

Unless Selby stopped in the middle of a headlock and pushed Kiernan's own blond hair back from his eyes.

Unless they both held their breath and looked at each other, like they were waiting for something big to happen, something they couldn't name, but something that seemed to weigh over them like the hope of rain from a pregnant cloud.

Selby closed his eyes, breaking the gravity of the moment, and no one was more surprised than Kiernan when *Kiernan* was the one who lunged forward and pressed their lips together.

And nobody was more surprised than Kiernan when Selby opened his mouth slightly and pushed back.

Kiernan closed his eyes, thinking *Oh. This is a kiss. It's nice. Selby's mouth feels good, doesn't it?*

They both pulled back and stood up, closer than they usually stood. Selby licked his lips and glanced over his shoulder at the stream. "I, uh… what if you didn't like me?" he asked baldly. "You… I mean, just because you liked boys didn't mean you'd like *me* that way." He shrugged. "It was easier to crush on your sister." A smile played with the corner of his mouth then, a sad one. "That's not so easy anymore."

Kiernan thought of Dean, the perfectly beautiful boy. He'd always known, hadn't he? Dean was too far away.

"No," he agreed. "Do you want to swim?"

Selby smiled, and he looked relieved. "God, yes. It'll be too cold soon!" He drew away, anxious to do something else.

Kiernan didn't blame him. Who wanted to think about kissing and crushes anyway? Because things were too grown-up right now; they hurt too much. The vision of Dean made him ache in his stomach, in his groin—at the same time it cut to the bone. Chelsea wasn't a horrible sister. She gave him rides to school and took him and Selby to the movies. She cooked dinner when their dad didn't get home in time and taught Kiernan how to make spaghetti. She'd been looking at Dean like he was perfect, amazing, the most beautiful boy in the world.

Kiernan couldn't think of him like that anymore, and a small part of his heart felt lost and sad.

But he and Selby had kissed, and that was glorious. Maybe live with that knowledge, let it sit tight in their hearts for a while. Maybe let it follow them through eighth grade to high school.

Maybe hold it to his chest, thinking about proms and night walks, and a moment to make a kiss deeper.

Maybe change the dream from Dean, who was far away, to Selby, who was stripping down to his undershorts to swim in the stream, his body stringy and freckled and pale in the golden sunshine.

The real most beautiful boy in the world.

AMY LANE is a mother of four and a compulsive knitter who writes because she can't silence the voices in her head. She adores cats, Chi-who-whats, knitting socks, and hawt menz, and she dislikes moths, cat boxes, and knuckle-headed macspazzmatrons. She is rarely found cooking, cleaning, or doing domestic chores, but she has been known to knit up an emergency hat/blanket/pair of socks for any occasion whatsoever, or sometimes for no reason at all. She writes in the shower, while at the gym, while taxiing children to soccer / dance / gymnastics / band oh my! and has learned from necessity to type like the wind. She lives in a spider-infested, crumbling house in a shoddy suburb and counts on her beloved Mate to keep her tethered to reality—which he does, while keeping her cell phone charged as a bonus. She's been married for twenty-plus years and still believes in Twu Wuv, with a capital Twu and a capital Wuv, and she doesn't see any reason at all for that to change.

Website: www.greenshill.com

Blog: www.writerslane.blogspot.com

E-mail: amylane@greenshill.com

Facebook: www.facebook.com/amy.lane.167

Twitter: @amymaclane

Also from HARMONY INK PRESS

FIRST TIME FOR
EVERYTHING

A HARMONY INK PRESS ANTHOLOGY

http://www.harmonyinkpress.com

Also from HARMONY INK PRESS

A HARMONY INK PRESS ANTHOLOGY

HARMONIOUS
HEARTS

http://www.harmonyinkpress.com

Also by GENE GANT

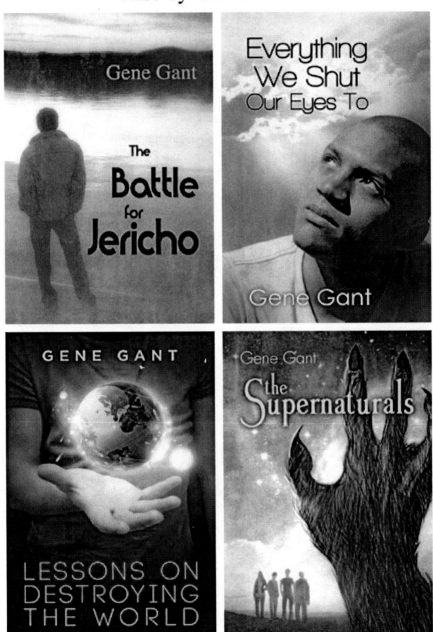

http://www.harmonyinkpress.com

Also by JOHN GOODE

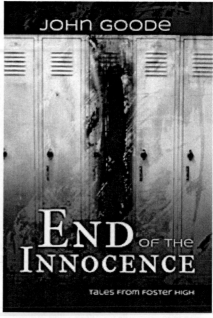

http://www.harmonyinkpress.com

Also by JOHN GOODE

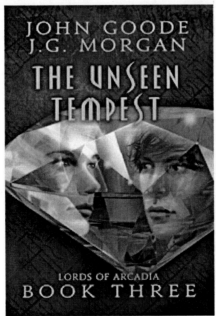

http://www.harmonyinkpress.com

Also by SAM KADENCE

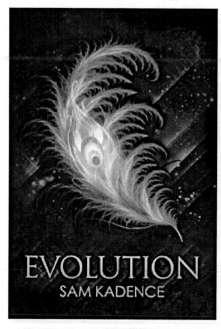

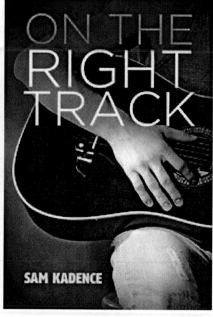

http://www.harmonyinkpress.com

Also by AMY LANE

http://www.harmonyinkpress.com

Also by ZOE LYNNE

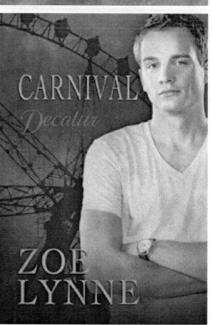

http://www.harmonyinkpress.com

Also by JO RAMSEY

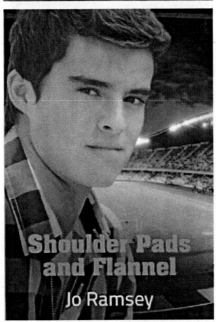

http://www.harmonyinkpress.com

FOR MORE
OF THE BEST
LGBTQ+ YA FICTION

Harmony Ink

VISIT

HARMONYINKPRESS.COM

CPSIA information can be obtained
at www.ICGtesting.com
Printed in the USA
FFOW05n2032201014

9 781632 169402